Dora's Chilly Day

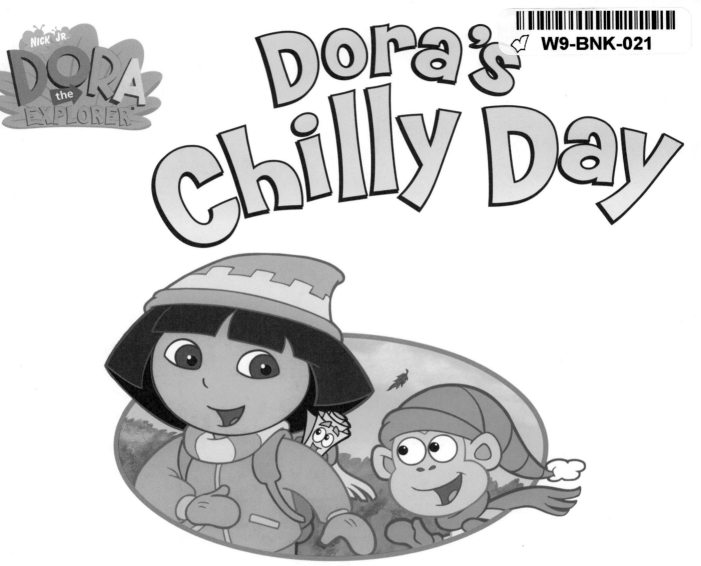

by Kiki Thorpe   illustrated by Steven Savitsky

Simon Spotlight/Nick Jr.

New York   London   Toronto   Sydney

Based on the TV series *Dora the Explorer*® as seen on Nick Jr.®

SIMON SPOTLIGHT
An imprint of Simon & Schuster Children's Publishing Division
1230 Avenue of the Americas, New York, New York 10020
Copyright © 2004 Viacom International Inc. All rights reserved.
NICKELODEON, NICK JR., *Dora the Explorer*, and all related titles, logos, and characters are
registered trademarks of Viacom International Inc.
All rights reserved, including the right of reproduction in whole or in part in any form.
SIMON SPOTLIGHT and colophon are registered trademarks of Simon & Schuster, Inc.
Manufactured in the United States of America
First Edition
2 4 6 8 10 9 7 5 3 1
ISBN 0-689-86795-6

¡Hola! Today Boots and I are visiting *Abuela's* house.

Brrr! It's chilly today. *Abuela* is going to make a chilly day surprise! She needs milk, sugar, and chocolate . . .

Uh-oh! *Abuela* has run out of chocolate. She can't make the surprise without it!

Wait! I know where we can get some: the Chocolate Tree! Boots and I will go to the Chocolate Tree to get some chocolate for *Abuela*. Will you help us? Great!

First we'll need something to help us stay warm outside. Let's look in Backpack. Say "Backpack!"

Do you see something that will keep us warm? Right! Some mittens and hats will help us stay warm! Now we're ready to go and see our friend the Chocolate Tree.

Let's ask Map what the best way is to the Chocolate Tree.

Map says that to get to the Chocolate Tree we have to go over the Troll Bridge and through the Nutty Forest. *¡Vámonos!* Let's go!

Brrr! The wind sure is strong. What a chilly day!
Look, there's Diego. I wonder what Diego likes to do on a chilly day . . .

Diego is bringing some straw to Mama Blue Bird so she can build a nice warm nest for her Blue Bird babies. Nice work, Diego! Come on! We're almost at the Troll Bridge.

We made it to the Troll Bridge. And there's the Grumpy Old Troll. What do you think the Grumpy Old Troll likes to do on a chilly day?

The Grumpy Old Troll likes to make up new riddles! And he has a special chilly day riddle for us:

"*This riddle is tricky. You'll have to think twice. When water freezes, it turns into . . .*"

That's a hard one. Do you know the answer?

Ice, right! Yay! We solved the Troll's riddle. Now we can cross the Troll Bridge!

Look! There's our friend the Big Red Chicken. I wonder what the Big Red Chicken likes to do on a chilly day . . .

The Big Red Chicken is knitting a big red scarf! That will help him stay nice and warm.

Do you remember where we go next? That's right—
the Nutty Forest! *Adiós*, Big Red Chicken!

Uh-oh. That's a very mucky mud puddle. We have to cross it to get to the Nutty Forest. Do you see a way to get to the other side?

We can use those stepping-stones.
Good thinking!

Mmmm! What's that delicious smell? It's coming from Tico's Tree House!

Tico likes to bake Nutty Butter Cookies on a chilly day. And he has some cookies for us! *Gracias*, Tico. Come on, let's hurry. We're almost there!

We made it! *Hola,* Chocolate Tree! *Abuela* needs three pieces of chocolate for her surprise. Do you see three pieces?

I can't wait to see what the chilly day surprise is. Let's hurry back to *Abuela's* house. Remember to keep an eye out for Swiper. That sneaky fox will try to swipe our chocolate. If you see him, say "Swiper, no swiping!"

Hooray! We brought the chocolate home to _Abuela._ Now she can make the chilly day surprise.

Abuela taught us a special chocolate song in Spanish. While *Abuela* mixes in the chocolate, we can help her by singing. Will you sing with us? Great!

¡Bate, bate—chocolate!
¡Bate, bate—chocolate!

Abuela's chilly day surprise is hot chocolate. *¡Delicioso!* I love drinking hot chocolate on a chilly day.
What do *you* like to do on a chilly day?

NICK JR.
DORA the EXPLORER

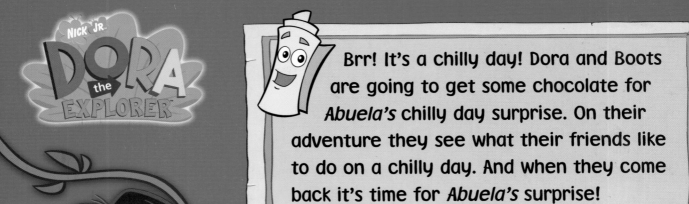

Brr! It's a chilly day! Dora and Boots are going to get some chocolate for *Abuela's* chilly day surprise. On their adventure they see what their friends like to do on a chilly day. And when they come back it's time for *Abuela's* surprise!

Look for more books about Dora the Explorer at your favorite store!

Look for Nick Jr.
Books in Spanish

Play to Learn™   NICKELODEON®

SIMON SPOTLIGHT / NICK JR.
Simon & Schuster, New York
VISIT OUR WEB SITES:
www.SimonSaysKids.com and www.nickjr.com

PRICE $3.99
DORAS CHILLY DAY

447 A

DORA EXPLO 1171 8x8spinner — G1
7587202 QP   6 91504 # SIMJ   2
702—01A 4205672

Big Sister Dora!

adapted by Alison Inches
illustrated by Dave Aikins

#13

NICK JR.

DORA the EXPLORER®

Big Sister Dora!

adapted by Alison Inches

illustrated by Dave Aikins

Simon Spotlight/Nick Jr.

New York   London   Toronto   Sydney

Based on the TV series *Dora the Explorer* ® as seen on Nick Jr.®

SIMON SPOTLIGHT
An imprint of Simon & Schuster Children's Publishing Division
1230 Avenue of the Americas, New York, New York 10020
Copyright © 2005 Viacom International Inc. All rights reserved.
NICKELODEON, NICK JR., *Dora the Explorer,* and all related titles, logos, and characters
are registered trademarks of Viacom International Inc.
All rights reserved, including the right of reproduction in whole or in part in any form.
SIMON SPOTLIGHT and colophon are registered trademarks of Simon & Schuster, Inc.
Manufactured in the United States of America
10 9 8 7 6 5 4
ISBN 0-689-87846-X